U0052657

英語聽&說

入門篇

白野伊津夫
Lisa A. Stefani
沈薇 譯

著

CD
BOOK

LISTENING & SPEAKING
STRATEGIES
INTRODUCTORY COURSE

三民書局

前　言

　　世界上有許多劃時代的大事及偉大的發明都是「逆向思考」所帶來的成果。例如現代日常生活中不可或缺的「電燈」，在古代是必須燃燒東西，即藉由燃燒氧氣、利用氧產生「光」，才能使煤油燈之類的器具發光照明；發明大王愛迪生則發明電燈泡，透過不需燃燒氧氣的過程產生光,這可說是一種逆向思考的偉大發明。由於這項發明，使得現代人即使在夜晚也能過著與白天無異的生活。

　　《英語聽＆說》這一系列書即是依據「逆向思考」的理念所企劃出來的語言學習書。本「入門篇」是此系列書的第一冊。我們之所以學習外語，是為了能夠流利地與外國人溝通，而傳統的英語學習方式也理所當然是以教「說英語」開始。不過，即使有為數眾多的人遵循傳統的英語學習方式，仍只有少數人能自由地以英語與人暢談。為了突破這種英語學習的瓶頸，本系列書特地引薦「聽英語」的學習法，期待能讓學習者盡快以流利的英語與人溝通。

　　從「聽」到「說」本來就是人類學習語言的自然過程。試想，若沒有母親在身邊長期不斷地說話引導，小孩根本無從學會說話。小孩原本不會說一字一語，是先默默聽母親講話，在約略懂得母親話裡的涵義之後，才不斷試著模仿說出。經過這樣的反覆練習後，小孩開始能流利地與大人溝通。我們即依據兒童學習語言的過程完成此系列書，各章皆由從「聽」(Listening) 開始，再到「說」(Speaking) 的結構組成。

　　經常可以聽到學習者抱怨：「能開口說一些些英語，但在聽的方面就是不行」，這就是傳統教學上注重「從說開始」的弊病。

由於不懂對方說什麼，所以內心會感到強烈的不安與害怕，不僅無法與外國人自在地聊天，相反地，還因受到相當大的挫折而痛苦不已。遇到這種瓶頸後，根本再也無法提高英語會話能力了。若是我們改變學習方式，「從聽開始」學習英語，相信不久即能聽懂外國人說的話，可以消除向來的不安與恐懼，愉悅地與他們對談，在往後的英語會話上也必定有很大的進步。

「從聽開始」學習的好處還不只這些。當我們的聽力提升之後，即能隨意捕捉身邊所聽到的英語，進而理解其涵義，如電視和廣播的外國新聞以及英語節目等，這些英語資訊大量地「輸入」(input) 到我們的腦海中，經儲存、吸收後，即可融合成自己的意見及感想，依不同的會話場景「輸出」(output) 出去。達到這個階段後，即能隨時與外國人暢所欲言，相信外國人士也會期待下一次與你的愉快對話。

在經濟及其他事物都已全球化進展的今日世界，英語早就是世界性的共通語言，是地球村中所有人的最佳溝通利器。衷心希望依逆向思考理念製作完成的此系列書能幫助各位精進英語會話能力，並在商場上無往不利，進而幫助世界公民理解彼此之間文化及語言上的差異。

白野伊津夫
Lisa A. Stefani

目 次

前言
本書使用方法

Chapter 1: Greeting（問候） 1

Chapter 2: Introduction（介紹） 6

Chapter 3: Asking For Permission（請求許可） 11

Chapter 4: Requests（提出要求） 16

Chapter 5: Asking Questions（詢問） 21

Chapter 6: Enjoying Food（享受美食） 26

Chapter 7: What Did You Do Today?（你今天做了什麼?） 32

Chapter 8: Is Dr. Johnson In Today?（請問強森博士在嗎?） 38

Chapter 9: Future Plans（未來計劃） 44

Chapter 10: Telephone Calls（打電話） 50

本書使用方法

本書共十章，各章分 Listening 及 Speaking 兩大部分，兩個部分再各由三個小單元組成。

Listening

最先出現的「Warm-up/Pre-questions」是測驗第一次聽完會話內容後的理解程度的選擇題，請聽完 CD 播放一次後立即作答。只要掌握會話的大概內容，得到正確的答案即可，不需在意細節或刻意熟習每個字句。由於是聽力的熱身運動，所以可以輕鬆面對。

「提升聽力的發音技巧」中會說明英語的發音原則，將有益於英語聽力的訓練。英語聽力確實會依所聽的量的多寡而有不同的進步，但光聽是不夠的，其進步不僅慢，甚至還可能會「原地踏步」。想要有效率且快速地提升聽力，就必須掌握正確的英語發音。這個單元旨在點明為什麼聽不懂及如何聽懂的方法，並提供練習題，測驗是否能掌握英語的發音原則及聽力是否有所提升。若有聽不懂的地方，可以多聽幾次 CD 以增加耳朵的靈敏度。

「Listening Quiz」是驗收成果測驗。在了解英語的發音、提升聽力之後，再聽一次會話，測驗能正確聽懂多少的會話內容。請利用之前學習的發音原則仔細聆聽，相信可以 100% 理解。無法正確回答時，請務必反覆聽 CD 直到徹底了解為止。

Speaking

一開始的「會話」(dialog) 可說是該章的重點，介紹並說明該章的主題內容。首先，請先默念該會話內容理解意思，若有不懂的地方再看「中譯」或「關鍵字」說明。接下來聽 CD，充分掌握英語的發音、節奏及語調後再發出聲音朗讀。朗讀時，最好是將自己融入為會話主角，並確認自己的英語是否與 CD 播放的英語一樣流暢。建議可以採取聽 CD 後朗誦、朗誦後聽 CD 的間歇式 (interval) 練習法學習。

若對發音有自信，也可以採用投影練習法 (shadow training)，這是緊跟著 CD 馬上覆誦的有效學習法。請確實跟隨 CD 自行朗誦，看看自己的發音是否接近外國人的母語。經過這一連串的練習，至少可誦唸 20 到 30 次的會話，相信必能幫助學習者脫口說出自然流利的英語。

「說法（代換、角色扮演）」中介紹並解說各章會話主題的基本及重要的語句表達方式，熟記以及活用這些語句將可大幅提升會話實力。首先請檢測是否了解英文語句的意義，再看「解說」釐清概念，也可以一併記下其他的相關語句。接下來仔細聽 CD 做「代換、角色扮演」的練習。「代換」練習是邊看基本句邊聽 CD 的代換詞句部分，再覆誦整句話，之後聆聽 CD 播放完整代換句的正確發音，請反覆練習直到可以說出流暢的英語句子來。「角色扮演」是視 CD 為談話對象的練習，先注意聆聽完整的對話示範，然後當聽到嗶一聲後說出適當的英語對應。剛開始可以看書說，但希望經過幾次練習後能不用看書而立即回答。

「實力測驗」是提供某一情境，讓學習者自我檢驗是否能就所學說出流利的英語對應。目的並非要求「正確的回答」，而是能以輕鬆的態度立刻說出自己想表達的話，讓對方了解，即使是稍微不正確的英語也無妨。最後會提供一個參考解答。

Greeting 問 候

Listening

Warm-up / Pre-questions

請聽《Track 1》的會話後回答下面問題。

這兩個人正在做什麼?
(A) 彼此打招呼
(B) 交報告
(C) 用餐

解答 (A)

提升聽力的發音技巧

1. 同化……緊鄰的音合成一個音 － And you? －
英語中,有緊鄰的兩個音互相影響而形成一個音的現象。例如:
[d] + [j] → [dʒ]——and you / did you
[t] + [j] → [tʃ]——don't you

練習 1

請聽《Track 2》並在括弧內填入正確答案。
1. ( ) ( ) call me last night?
2. I ( ) ( ) help.
3. ( ) ( ) sit down?

解答

1. (Did) (you) call me last night?
2. I (need) (your) help.
3. (Won't) (you) sit down?
（請坐）

2. 弱讀音 (1)…… be 動詞 － we're finished －

be 動詞通常發弱音。

am [ˋæm] → [əm] / are [ˋɑr] → [ɚ] / is [ˋɪz] → [z] [s] /
was [ˋwɑz] → [wəz] / were [ˋwɝ] → [wɚ]

練習 2

請聽《Track 3》並在括弧內填入正確答案。

1. You (   ) welcome.
2. She (   ) surprised at the news.
3. There (   ) still many problems.

解答

1. You (are) welcome.
2. She (was) surprised at the news.
3. There (are) still many problems.

Listening Quiz

請聽《Track 1》的會話後回答下面問題。

Jim 的報告什麼時候會完成？
(A) 星期一以前　　　(B) 星期三以前
(C) 星期四以前　　　(D) 下禮拜之前

解答　　　　　　　　　　　　　　　　　　(B)

Speaking

會話

 請再聽一次《Track 1》。

Jack: Hello, Jim. How are you doing today?

Jim: Really well, thank you. And you?

Jack: Great, thanks. How is your report coming?

Jim: Slowly, but I will be finished by Wednesday.

Jack: My report is taking a while to finish, too.

Jim: We should go out to dinner when we're finished.

Jack: Sounds great.

中譯

傑克：嗨，吉姆，今天過得好嗎？

吉姆：很不錯，謝謝！你呢？

傑克：我也很好，謝謝！你的報告進行得怎麼樣？

吉姆：目前進度偏慢，不過我會在星期三之前完成。

傑克：我的報告也還要一些時間才能完成。

吉姆：等報告完成後，我們一起吃頓飯慶祝一下吧！

傑克：好啊！

關鍵字

be finished　完成，結束

take a while　花費一些時間，要一會兒

Sounds great.　聽起來不錯。（It sounds great. 的省略）

問候的說法

請聽《Track 4》。

1. A: How are you today?

   B: I'm fine, thank you.

2. A: Good morning. How are you today?

   B: Fine, thank you. How are you?

3. A: How are you doing today?

   B: Really well, thank you. And you?

解說

● Good morning. 是中午前使用的問候語，也可以簡略只說 Morning. 替代。

● 當有人對你說 How are you? 時，別只用 I'm fine, thank you. 回答，應該再加上 How are you? 或 And you? 回應才更有禮貌。

練習 1【代換】

請隨《Track 5》做代換練習。

1. How are you, Bill?

   > Meg?
   > Jack?
   > Patty?
   > Don?

2. How are you doing, Betty?

   > John?
   > Cathy?
   > Eric?
   > Kate?

練習 2【角色扮演】

請隨《Track 6》在嗶一聲後唸出灰色部分的句子。

1. A: How are you today, Jim?

   B: I'm fine, thank you.

2. A: Good morning, Bill. How are you today?

   B: Fine, thank you. How are you?

3. A: How are you doing today?

   B: Really well, thank you. And you?

實力測驗

有一天你和朋友 Harry 在路上不期而遇，Harry 先開口說 "Hi, how are you doing?"，這時你要如何用英語回應呢？

參考解答 　　　　　　　　Really well, thank you. And you?

<table>
<tr><td>Chapter
2</td><td>**Introduction**</td><td>介　紹</td></tr>
</table>

Listening

Warm-up / Pre-questions

請聽《Track 7》的會話後回答下面問題。

介紹 Davis 和 Amy 認識的人是誰?
(A) Amy 的秘書
(B) Amy 的老闆
(C) Davis 的同事

解答	(B)

提升聽力的發音技巧

1. 縮略字 (1)……結合兩個單字　－ I'm －
英語經常會使用縮略字,如 I'm 即是 I am 的縮寫。不論是印刷或手寫的文字,只要看一眼,我們就可以認出 I'm 這個縮略字。但在實際會話中是沒有文字可以做判斷的,所以平時必須加強熟悉縮略字的發音。
1.名詞‧代名詞＋be 動詞　I'm happy. / She's nice. / Jim's at work.
2.名詞‧代名詞＋助動詞　You'll / Jack'll / I'd like

練習 1

請聽《Track 8》並在括弧內填入正確答案。

1. (　　　　) quite fine.
2. (　　　　) very angry.
3. (　　　　) be 25 dollars.

解答

1. (They're) quite fine.
2. (Mary's) very angry.
3. (That'll) be 25 dollars.
   (那個是 25 美元)

2. 弱讀音 (2)……介系詞

介系詞通常發弱音。

at [`æt] → [ət] / for [`fɔr] → [fɚ] / of [`ɑv] → [əv] /
to [`tu] → [tə] / from [`frɑm] → [frəm]

練習 2

請聽《Track 9》並在括弧內填入正確答案。

1. She's a friend (   ) mine.
2. It's nice (   ) meet you.
3. I often work (   ) night.

解答

1. She's a friend (of) mine.
2. It's nice (to) meet you.
3. I often work (at) night.

Listening Quiz

請聽《Track 7》的會話後回答下面問題。

Davis 和 Amy 在期待什麼?

(A) 休假　　　　　　(B) 迎接新同事聚餐
(C) 一起工作　　　　(D) 和老闆一起用餐

解答　　　　　　　　　　　　　　　　　　(C)

Speaking

會話

 請再聽一次《Track 7》。

Steve: Hello, Amy. I'd like you to meet the new director of accounting, Ms. Davis. Ms. Davis, this is Amy, my secretary.

Ms. Davis: Hello, Amy. I'm glad to meet you.

Amy: Hello. Ms. Davis. I'm very happy to meet you, too.

Steve: Amy will assist you with invoicing every month.

Ms. Davis: Good. I'll be happy to have your assistance.

Amy: Thank you. I look forward to working with you.

中譯

史帝夫： 嗨，艾美。讓我為妳介紹我們的新會計部經理，戴維斯小姐。戴維斯小姐，這位是我的秘書艾美。

戴維斯： 艾美，妳好，幸會。

艾　美： 妳好，戴維斯小姐，很高興認識妳。

史帝夫： 艾美往後每個月會協助妳開發票。

戴維斯： 太好了，很高興有妳來幫我。

艾　美： 謝謝! 我也很期待和妳一起工作。

關鍵字

invoice　　開發票（商品發貨單）

look forward to　　期待，盼望

介紹的說法

 請聽《Track 10》。

---

1. A: Ms. Harris, may I introduce my friend, Mr. Foster?

   B: How do you do, Mr. Foster? I'm glad to meet you.

   C: How do you do, Ms. Harris? I'm glad to meet you, too.

2. A: Jack, I'd like you to meet my new client, Mr. Owen.

   B: I'm very pleased to know you, Mr. Owen.

   C: I'm very happy to meet you, too, Jack.

3. A: Let me introduce myself. My name is Nancy Jones.

   B: How do you do, Nancy? My name is Alice Brown.

解說
- 介紹的對象有男女雙方時，應先將男性介紹給女性認識；若地位及年齡有相當差距時，則先將地位低、年紀小的人介紹給地位高或年紀大的人。
- 介紹客戶與公司同事認識時，應先將同事介紹給客戶；介紹時，也必須說出姓名，如果只說 I'd like you to meet my client. 的話會很失禮。
- 自我介紹時也可以說 May I introduce myself?。

練習 1【代換】

 請隨《Track 11》做代換練習。

1. Ms. Harris, may I introduce my friend, Mr. Foster?

   my sister, Nancy?

   my teacher, Mr. Scott?

   my new secretary, Helen Anderson?

   my colleague, Jim Taylor?

2. How do you do, Jack? I'm glad to meet you.

> Mr. Williams? I'm very happy to meet you.
> Miss Martin? I'm pleased to know you.
> Mrs. Cole? I'm delighted to know you, too.
> Mr. Davis? It's a great honor to meet you.

練習 2【角色扮演】

 請隨《Track 12》在嗶一聲後唸出灰色部分的句子。

1. A: Mrs. Brown, may I introduce my friend, Miss Wilson?

   B: How do you do, Miss Wilson? I'm glad to meet you.

   C: How do you do, Mrs. Brown? I'm glad to meet you, too.

2. A: Jim, I'd like you to meet my new client, Mr. Miller.

   B: I'm very pleased to know you, Mr. Miller.

   C: I'm very happy to meet you, too, Jim.

3. A: Let me introduce myself. My name is Susan Hill.

   B: How do you do, Susan? My name is Rose Taylor.

實力測驗

請練習將大學時代的朋友 Richard Nelson 介紹給公司老闆 Miller
認識。

參考解答	Mr. Miller, may I introduce my friend, Richard Nelson? He and I went to college together.

Chapter 3

Asking For Permission　請求許可

Listening

Warm-up / Pre-questions

請聽《Track 13》的會話後回答下面問題。

對話中的女子想跟 Mark 借什麼?
(A) 電腦
(B) 植物盆栽
(C) 數位相機

解答 (C)

提升聽力的發音技巧

1. 連音 (1)……流利地連結單字　− go right ahead −
雖然英語的單字是一個一個分開寫,但在實際會話中,會將單字的尾音與下一個單字的首音連起來一起發,聽起來像是一個單字的連續發音。因此,單字的區隔變得不明顯。聽到的單字音間隔往往和書寫單字的間隔有差異。
[p] [b] [t] [d] [k] [g] 的音 + 母音　go right ahead → gorightahead
[m] [n] [g] 的音 + 母音　return it → returnit / as soon as → as soonas

練習 1

請聽《Track 14》並在括弧內填入正確答案。

1. (　　)(　　)(　　) the table.
2. I (　　)(　　)(　　).
3. (　　)(　　)(　　) doing here?

解答　　　　1. (Put) (it) (on) the table.　　2. I (read) (about) (it).
　　　　　　3. (What) (am) (I) doing here?

2. 弱讀音 (3)……代名詞 －May I use your digital camera?－
代名詞通常發弱音。

me [ˋmi] → [mɪ] / you [ˋju] → [jʊ], your [ˋjʊr] → [jʊr] /
he [ˋhi] → [hɪ], his [ˋhɪz] → [hɪz], him [ˋhɪm] → [hɪm] /
she [ˋʃi] → [ʃɪ], her [ˋhɝ] → [hɚ] / we [ˋwi] → [wɪ], our [aʊr] → [ɑr],
us [ˋʌs] → [əs] / their [ðɛr] → [ðɚ], them [ˋðɛm] → [ðəm]

練習 2

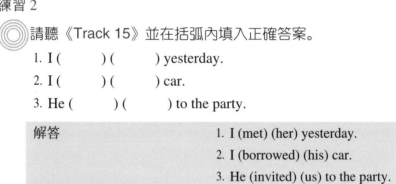

請聽《Track 15》並在括弧內填入正確答案。

　　1. I (　　　) (　　　) yesterday.

　　2. I (　　　) (　　　) car.

　　3. He (　　　) (　　　) to the party.

解答　　　　　　　　　1. I (met) (her) yesterday.

　　　　　　　　　　　2. I (borrowed) (his) car.

　　　　　　　　　　　3. He (invited) (us) to the party.

Listening Quiz

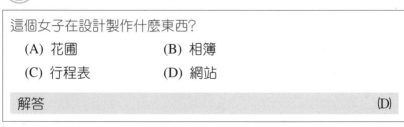

請聽《Track 13》的會話後回答下面問題。

這個女子在設計製作什麼東西？

　(A) 花圃　　　　　　(B) 相簿

　(C) 行程表　　　　　(D) 網站

解答　　　　　　　　　　　　　　　　　　　(D)

Speaking

會話

請再聽一次《Track 13》。

A: Hi, Mark. May I borrow your digital camera a moment?

B: Sure. Go right ahead. Here it is.

A: Thank you. I'll return it as soon as I finish taking pictures of the flowers in the garden. I'm making a website about flowers.

B: That sounds very interesting. Could I see it when it's done?

A: Yes, of course. You'll be the first person to see it.

B: Great. I can't wait to see it.

中譯

A： 嗨，馬克，可以跟你借一下數位相機嗎？

B： 沒問題。東西在這，妳拿去吧。

A： 謝謝。我一拍完花園裡的花就會立刻還你。我正在設計一個以花為主題的網站。

B： 聽起來蠻有趣的。網站完成後可以讓我參觀一下嗎？

A： 當然可以。你將會是第一位訪客。

B： 太棒了，我已經等不及要看了。

關鍵字

a moment　　一會兒，片刻

website　　網站（全球資訊網的主機站）

sound　　聽起來

can't wait to　　等不及了（很想，很渴望，形容迫不及待的樣子）

請求許可的說法

請聽《Track 16》。

1. A: May I open the window?
   B: Sure. Go right ahead.
2. A: Could I use your car this afternoon?
   B: Yes, of course.
3. A: Do you mind if I sit here?
   B: No, not at all.

解說

● May I～? 及 Can I～? 皆是請求許可的常用句型。

● Could I～? 是比 Can I～? 更為禮貌的句型。

● Do you mind if I～? 也是請求許可的句型。允許對方的要求時，通常可以回答 No, not at all. / Certainly not. / Of course not. 等；若不允許則使用 I'm afraid you can't～ 或 I'm sorry, but it's not allowed here. 等較為客氣的說法。

練習 1【代換】

請隨《Track 17》做代換練習。

1. May I come in?

   take a break?
   use your phone?
   speak to you?
   ask you a question?

2. Do you mind if I smoke?

> leave now?
> don't come with you?
> turn on the TV?
> cancel the appointment?

練習 2【角色扮演】

 請隨《Track 18》在嗶一聲後唸出灰色部分的句子。

1. A: May I close the window?

   B: Sure. Go right ahead.

2. A: Could I talk with you?

   B: Yes, of course.

3. A: Do you mind if I put it here?

   B: No, not at all.

實力測驗

跟同事 Jack 借來一閱的報告非常有意思，你很想影印一份留存，這時該如何請求他的允許呢？

參考解答　　　　　　　Jack, may I photocopy this report?

Requests 提出要求

Listening

Warm-up / Pre-questions

請聽《Track 19》的會話後回答下面問題。

這位男士想去哪裡?

(A) 音樂廳

(B) Hall 先生的辦公室

(C) 服務台

解答   (B)

提升聽力的發音技巧

1. 連音 (2)……連結單字 —His office is on the fifth floor.—

His office is on 唸快點會聽起來像 [hɪ/sɔ/fɪ/sɪ/son]，這是由於 [s] 和 [z] 的音容易和下個單字的母音合起來唸的緣故。[r] 和 [l] 也會和其後單字的母音連結。

[f] [v] [θ] [ð] [s] [z] [ʃ] [ʒ] 的音 + 母音 I have a book./This is a book.

[r] [l] 的音 + 母音   Here is a book. / Shall I open the door?

練習 1

請聽《Track 20》並在括弧內填入正確答案。

1. The (   ) (   ) melting.

2. I'll (   ) (   ) now.

3. Will you (   ) (   ) the form?

2. 弱讀音 (4)……冠詞 － Is there an elevator? －

冠詞通常發弱音。

a [e] → [ə] / an [`æn] → [ən] / the [`ði] → [ðə]

練習 2

◎ 請聽《Track 21》並在括弧內填入正確答案。

1. (　　　) (　　　) (　　　) typist.

2. Let's go (　　　) (　　　) (　　　) (　　　).

3. Turn (　　　) (　　　) (　　　) now.

解答	1. (She's) (an) (excellent) typist.
	2. Let's go (to) (see) (a) (movie).
	3. Turn (on) (the) (light) now.

Listening Quiz

◎ 請聽《Track 19》的會話後回答下面問題。

Hall 先生的辦公室在幾樓？

(A) 2 樓 　　　　　 (B) 5 樓

(C) 10 樓 　　　　　 (D) 15 樓

解答 　　　　　　　　　　　　　　　　　　(B)

Speaking

會話

 請再聽一次《Track 19》。

A: Excuse me.

B: Yes?

A: Could you please tell me where Mr. Hall's office is?

B: Certainly. Mr. Hall's office is on the fifth floor. Suite 502.

A: Is there an elevator?

B: Yes, it's at the end of the passage.

A: Thank you very much.

B: You're welcome.

中譯

A： 打擾一下。

B： 有什麼事嗎?

A： 可以麻煩你告訴我霍爾先生的辦公室在哪兒嗎?

B： 沒問題,霍爾先生的辦公室在 5 樓 502 室。

A： 請問有電梯嗎?

B： 有,就在這條走廊的盡頭。

A： 非常謝謝你。

B： 不用客氣。

關鍵字

the fifth floor　第五層,5 樓

suite　套房（通常是指飯店內設備完善的房間,但也可以用來指辦公的地方）

請求的說法

請聽《Track 22》。

1. A: Would you please pass me the salt?
   B: Sure. Here you are.
2. A: Could you please call me again later?
   B: All right. What time shall I call?
3. A: Would you mind turning off your cellular phone?
   B: Of course not.

解說
● Would you please～? 是請求他人做某事的句型，比 Will you please～? 更客氣。
● Could you please～? 也是比 Can you please～? 更客氣的說法。
● Would you mind +V.ing? 同樣也是請求句型，比 Do you mind +V.ing? 更為客氣，聽話者可以用 Not at all. 或 Of course not. 回答。

練習 1【代換】

請隨《Track 23》做代換練習。

1. Could you please call a taxi for me?
   press five?
   help me with this work?
   tell me his phone number again?
   tell him that Mike called again?

2. Would you mind putting your bag on the rack?
                               making a hotel reservation for me?
                               mailing this package for me?
                               moving up a little bit?
                               turning down the TV?

練習 2【角色扮演】

 請隨《Track 24》在嗶一聲後唸出灰色部分的句子。

1. A: Would you please pass me the pepper?
   B: Sure. Here you are.

2. A: Could you please come again later?
   B: All right. What time shall I come?

3. A: Would you mind waiting for a few minutes?
   B: Of course not.

實力測驗

> 辦公室的電話鈴聲忽然響起，此時的你正忙著影印資料而走不開，
> 所以打算麻煩同事 John 幫忙接一下電話，你應該如何開口拜託他
> 呢？

參考解答　　　　　John, could you please answer the phone?

<table>
<tr><td>Chapter
5</td><td>**Asking Questions**</td><td>詢　問</td></tr>
</table>

Listening

Warm-up / Pre-questions

◎ 請聽《Track 25》的會話後回答下面問題。

Mike 今天為什麼沒去上班?

(A) 因為是假日

(B) 因為正流行感冒

(C) 因為身體不舒服

解答　　　　　　　　　　　　　　　　　　(C)

提升聽力的發音技巧

1. 省略音 (1)⋯⋯因後接的音而省略不發的現象

— right now —

英文書寫時雖然有字母,但在實際會話中,會依後接的音而有本身發音消失的現象。例如 right now 的 [t] 和 [n] 兩者在發音時,由於舌頭發音的位置相同, [t] 的音會不見,產生一個「停頓」,而後轉成發 [n] 的音。

[p] [t] [k] [b] [d] [g] 等的塞音 + [l] [m] [n] 的音　　I'd like / send me

練習 1

◎ 請聽《Track 26》並在括弧內填入正確答案。

1. Will you (　　　) (　　　) some money?

2. I (　　) (　　) this movie.

3. It's (　　) (　　).

解答 1. Will you (lend) (me) some money?

2. I (don't) (like) this movie.　　3. It's (brand) (new).

2. 弱讀音 (5)……助動詞 ― I can drive. ―

助動詞通常發弱音。

do [ˋdu] → [du] / does [ˋdʌz] → [dəz] / can [ˋkæn] → [kən] /

could [ˋkʊd] → [kəd] / will [ˋwɪl] → [wəl] / would [ˋwʊd] → [wəd] /

shall [ˋʃæl] → [ʃəl] / should [ˋʃʊd] → [ʃəd] / must [ˋmʌst] → [məst] /

have [ˋhæv] → [həv] / has [ˋhæz] → [həs] / had [ˋhæd] → [həd]

練習 2

◎ 請聽《Track 27》並在括弧內填入正確答案。

1. I (　　) (　　) it myself.

2. How (　　) (　　) like your steak?

3. What (　　) (　　) done to her?

解答　　　　　1. I (can) (do) it myself.

2. How (would) (you) like your steak?

3. What (have) (you) done to her?

Listening Quiz

◎ 請聽《Track 25》的會話後回答下面問題。

Mike 正打算做什麼？

(A) 吃藥　　　　　　(B) 到醫院

(C) 吃早餐　　　　　(D) 打電話預約

解答　　　　　　　　　　　　　　　　　　　　(D)

Speaking

會話

 請再聽一次《Track 25》。

A: Aren't you going to work today, Mike?

B: No. I'm not feeling very well.

A: What seems to be the problem?

B: I have a headache and stomachache. Is the flu going around?

A: They say there is a bad flu going around. Are you going to see the doctor?

B: Yes. I'm going to call him to make an appointment right now.

A: Do you want me to drive you to the hospital?

B: No, thank you. I think I can drive there myself.

中譯

A： 麥克，你今天不用上班嗎?

B： 不上班，我身體不太舒服。

A： 哪裡不舒服?

B： 我頭痛、肚子也痛。最近是不是又開始流行感冒了?

A： 據說是有一波很厲害的感冒在流行。你要不要去看醫生?

B： 要，我正要打電話跟醫生約時間。

A： 需要我載你去醫院嗎?

B： 不用了，謝謝。我想我可以自己開車去醫院。

關鍵字

the flu 流行性感冒（influenza 的縮寫）

(be) going around （指疾病）正在流行，肆虐

詢問的說法

請聽《Track 28》。

1. A: Do you like to go to the movies?
   B: Yes, very much.
2. A: Are you going to take a taxi?
   B: No. I'm taking the subway.
3. A: What are you going to do?
   B: I'm going to call her.

解說

● Do you like to～? 是詢問「你喜歡～嗎」的句型。另外，如 Would you like to sit down? 句子中的 Would you like to～? 是「你想做～嗎」的問句用法，常用於勸誘或建議對方做某事。

● 針對對方未來「打算做～」的行為，會用 Are you going to～? 或 Will you～? 等疑問句型詢問。

● 詢問重點在於「什麼」之意時，會用開頭是 What～? 的問句。

練習 1【代換】

請隨《Track 29》做代換練習。

1. Do you want to take a break?

> to have lunch now?
> to go to the beach?
> me to wait here?
> me to take you there?

2. What happened?
   is bothering you?
   do you mean?
   do you think of this?
   do you want me to do?

練習 2【角色扮演】

請隨《Track 30》在嗶一聲後唸出灰色部分的句子。

1. A: Do you want to take a vacation?

   B: Yes, of course.

2. A: Are you going to go there by plane?

   B: No. I'm driving.

3. A: What are you going to do?

   B: I'm going to take a break.

實力測驗

看到同事 Nancy 神情疲憊、臉色不佳的模樣，這時候，你會如何對她表達關心之意呢？

參考解答　　　You don't look well, Nancy. What seems to be the problem?

Chapter 6	**Enjoying Food**	享受美食

==== Listening ====

Warm-up / Pre-questions

請聽《Track 31》的會話後回答下面問題。

這位女士正做完什麼事?

(A) 結束工作

(B) 用完餐

(C) 喝完咖啡

解答　　　　　　　　　　　　　　　　　　　　　(B)

提升聽力的發音技巧

1. 省略音 (2)……依後接的音而省略不發的現象

　－ chocolate cake －

塞音如 [t] [d] 等之後再接塞音時, 第一個塞音往往會消失不見。
如 chocolate cake 的發音應為 [ˈtʃɔklɪt kek], 但實際聽起來像是
[tʃɔ/kə/lɪ/ke/k]。另外, 塞音之後若接的是 [tʃ] [dʒ] 時, 實際上也
會聽不到前面塞音的音。

塞音 + 塞音　　chocolate cake / take care

塞音 + [tʃ] [dʒ] [tr] [dr]　　good choice / hot drink

練習 1

請聽《Track 32》並在括弧內填入正確答案。

　　1. I had a very (　　　) (　　　).

　　2. I'll (　　　) (　　　) of it.

3. I'll (   ) (   ).

解答

1. I had a very (good) (time).
2. I'll (take) (care) of it.
3. I'll (get) (dressed).

2. 弱讀音 (6)⋯⋯連接詞 － coffee and dessert －

連接詞通常發弱音。

and [`ænd] → [ənd] / but [`bʌt] → [bət] / or [`ɔr] → [ɚ] /
for [`fɔr] → [fɚ] / that [`ðæt] → [ðət] / as [`æz] → [əz]

練習 2

◎ 請聽《Track 33》並在括弧內填入正確答案。

1. I take (   ) (   ) (   ) in my coffee.
2. I like it, (   ) (   ) don't want it now.
3. Would you like (   ) (   ) (   )?

解答

1. I take (cream) (and) (sugar) in my coffee.
2. I like it, (but) (I) don't want it now.
3. Would you like (coffee) (or) (tea)?

Listening Quiz

◎ 請聽《Track 31》的會話後回答下面問題。

這位女士要喝什麼樣的咖啡?
(A) 只加奶精的咖啡　　　(B) 只放糖的咖啡
(C) 加奶精也加糖的咖啡　(D) 什麼都不加的黑咖啡

解答   (D)

Speaking

會話

 請再聽一次《Track 31》。

A: What a delicious meal!

B: Thank you. I'm glad that you enjoyed it. Can I get you some coffee and dessert now?

A: Coffee and dessert sound wonderful.

B: Would you like regular coffee or decaf?

A: I prefer regular coffee.

B: Would you like sugar or cream in your coffee?

A: No, thank you. I like it black.

B: All right. We have chocolate cake and lemon pie for dessert. Which one would you like?

A: I'd like lemon pie.

B: All right. I'll bring them right to you.

中譯

A: 真是美味的一餐!

B: 謝謝,很高興您喜歡。可以上咖啡與甜點了嗎?

A: 好啊,我正想要咖啡與甜點。

B: 您要一般的咖啡還是不含咖啡因的咖啡?

A: 我喜歡一般的咖啡。

B: 需要加糖或奶精嗎?

A: 謝謝,不需要。黑咖啡就好了。

B：好的。至於甜點方面，我們有巧克力蛋糕與檸檬派，請問您要點哪一樣？

A：我要檸檬派。

B：好的，我馬上為您送來。

關鍵字

decaf　　無咖啡因的咖啡

prefer　　偏好，比較喜歡　　prefer A (to B)　　喜愛 A（甚於 B）

black　　純的，不加奶精的（有時亦指不加糖的）

感嘆句及表示喜好的說法

◎請聽《Track 34》。

1. A: What a delicious meal!

   B: Thank you. I'm glad you enjoyed it.

2. A: How beautiful this birthday cake is!

   B: Thank you. It should taste good.

3. A: Would you like regular coffee or decaf?

   B: I prefer regular coffee.

解說

● 以 What 起始的感嘆句，通常後接「(a / an) 形容詞 + 名詞」；也可以後接主詞及動詞，例如：What a delicious meal it was!。

● 以 How 起始的感嘆句，通常後接形容詞或副詞。

● 兩個事物中，喜歡一個甚於另一個時，可用 prefer 表達，通常採用 prefer A to B 的句型，等同於 like A better than B。

練習 1【代換】

請隨《Track 35》做代換練習。

1. What a tasty cake!

   a good pizza!
   delicious soup!
   a nice ice cream this is!
   a juicy steak this is!

2. How nice this chicken tastes!

   lovely this pie smells!
   pretty this birthday cake is!
   tender this steak is!
   delicious this melon smells!

練習 2【角色扮演】

請隨《Track 36》在嗶一聲後唸出灰色部分的句子。

1. A: What a delicious pizza!

   B: Thank you. Would you like another slice?

2. A: Here's your coffee.

   B: Thank you. How nice this coffee smells!

3. A: Would you like tea or coffee?

   B: I prefer coffee. Thank you.

實力測驗

你的朋友 Mary 為你做了個蘋果派,嚐了一口,又香又濃的酸甜滋味真是美味極了,你要如何表達讚美之意呢?

參考解答　　　　　What a delicious apple pie this is! You're a great cook.

Listening

Warm-up / Pre-questions

請聽《Track 37》的會話後回答下面問題。

> 這位女士今天做了什麼事?
> (A) 看畫展
> (B) 看電影
> (C) 買東西
>
> 解答 (C)

提升聽力的發音技巧

1. 連音 (3)⋯⋯連結單字 — It's incredibly huge. —

It's incredibly huge. 聽起來像是 [ɪ/tsɪn/krɛdəblɪ/hjudʒ],這是由於 [ts] 的音和後接的母音合起來唸的緣故。另外 [dz] 和 [tʃ] [dʒ] 也會和後接的母音連結。

[ts] [dz] [tʃ] [dʒ] 的音 + 母音 It's in the box.

練習 1

請聽《Track 38》並在括弧內填入正確答案。

1. ( ) ( ).

2. ( ) ( ) very expensive.

3. Everyone, ( ) ( ) ready.

解答 1. (It's) (important).　　2. (Diamonds) (are) very expensive.
　　　 3. Everyone, (lunch) (is) ready.

2. 不易區別的音 ⑴…… [v] 和 [b]　　—I bought a vest.—

英語有很多類似且難以區別的音。不過只要仔細多聽幾次，一定能夠抓住每個音的特質，清楚分辨其間的微妙差異。

[v] vs. [b]　　vest vs. best / vow vs. bow / vote vs. boat / vend vs. bend

[f] vs. [h]　　fit vs. hit / feel vs. heel / fall vs. hall / fire vs. hire

[s] vs. [θ]　　mouse vs. mouth / worse vs. worth / force vs. fourth

練習 2

◎ 請聽《Track 39》並在括弧內填入正確答案。

1. He (　　　) twice. / He (　　　) twice.

2. He was (　　) recently. / He was (　　) recently.

3. He has a big (　　) . / He has a big (　　).

解答　　　1. He (bowed) twice. / He (vowed) twice.
　　　　　2. He was (fired) recently. / He was (hired) recently.
　　　　　3. He has a big (mouth). / He has a big (mouse).

Listening Quiz

◎ 請聽《Track 37》的會話後回答下面問題。

這位女士買了什麼東西？

　(A) 帽子、背心和鞋子　　(B) 鞋子、毛衣和背心

　(C) 大衣、背心和裙子　　(D) 鞋子、毛衣和休閒褲

解答　　　.　　　　　　　　　　　　　　　(B)

Speaking

會話

 請再聽一次《Track 37》。

A: What did you do today?

B: I went shopping.

A: Really? Where did you go?

B: To the new mall in New Port.

A: Oh, I heard about it. It's the biggest mall in California, isn't it?

B: Yes, it is. It's incredibly huge.

A: What did you buy?

B: I bought a sweater, a vest, and a pair of shoes. What did you do today?

A: I went to the Powell Museum. They are exhibiting some of Picasso's paintings now.

B: That's right. I'm planning to go there next week. Did you enjoy the paintings?

A: Yes, very much.

中譯

A：妳今天做了什麼？

B：我去逛街了。

A：真的？妳去哪裡逛街？

B：我去了新港新開的購物中心逛街。

A：聽說那是全加州最大的購物中心，對吧？

B：沒錯，大到令人難以置信。

A：妳買了什麼？

B：我買了一件毛衣、一件背心和一雙鞋子。那你今天做了什麼呢？

A：我去參觀波威爾博物館，那裡正在展出一些畢卡索的畫作。

B：沒錯，我計畫下個禮拜去那裡參觀。你喜歡那些畫嗎？

A：非常喜歡！

關鍵字

go shopping　去逛街，去購物
mall　購物中心，大型商場

行為的說法

請聽《Track 40》。

1. A: What did you do today?

   B: I went shopping.

2. A: I went to the new mall in New Port.

   B: Oh really? It's the biggest mall in California, isn't it?

3. A: I went to the motor show.

   B: I'm planning to go there next week.

解說

● go + V.ing 是「去做～」的意思，例如：go swimming（去游泳），go hiking（去遠足）等。

● biggest 是 big 的最高級，比較級則是 bigger。比較級的用法是 Jim is bigger than Tom.；最高級的用法則是 Jim is the biggest boy in the class.。必須留意兩者的差別。

● 針對未來的行為，除了用 I will / I'm going to 表達之外，也可以說成 I'm planning to ～。

練習 1【代換】

請隨《Track 41》做代換練習。

1. I went shopping today.

> swimming today.
> fishing today.
> hiking yesterday.
> skiing over the weekend.

2. I'm planning to see the musical tomorrow.

> go to the exhibition tomorrow.
> go to the concert on Friday.
> visit my mother over the weekend.
> take a trip to Europe this summer.

練習 2【角色扮演】

請隨《Track 42》在嗶一聲後唸出灰色部分的句子。

1. A: What did you do today?

   B: I went surfing with my friends.

2. A: I had dinner at Atlantic Grill yesterday.

   B: Oh really? It's the best restaurant in town, isn't it?

3. A: I went to Venice Beach today.

   B: I'm planning to go there on Friday.

實力測驗

你和死黨們打完保齡球後各自回家，一進門正巧接到朋友 Tom 的
電話，他問你 What did you do today? 時，你會如何回答？

參考解答   I went bowling with my friends.

| Chapter 8 | Is Dr. Johnson In Today? | 請問強森博士在嗎？ |

Listening

Warm-up / Pre-questions

請聽《Track 43》的會話後回答下面問題。

Johnson 博士現在在哪裡？

(A) 會議室

(B) 辦公室

(C) 家裡

解答   (A)

提升聽力的發音技巧

1. 縮略字 (2)……結合兩個單字 － won't / isn't －

否定字 not 前接助動詞及 be 動詞時，通常會變成縮寫的形式，如 won't 或 isn't。

1. 助動詞 + not   will not → won't / can not → can't / must not → mustn't / should not → shouldn't / would not → wouldn't

2. be 動詞 + not   isn't / aren't / wasn't / weren't

練習 1

請聽《Track 44》並在括弧內填入正確答案。

1. Supper (　　　) be ready till seven o'clock.

2. You (　　　) drink too much.

3. It (　　　) so difficult.

1. Supper (won't) be ready till seven o'clock.

2. You (shouldn't) drink too much.

3. It (wasn't) so difficult.

2. 不易區別的音 (2)…… [ʃ] 和 [s]　— she vs. sea —

[ʃ] 和 [s] 也是類似又難以分辨的音，例如 she 和 sea，sheet 和 seat，必須小心區別，可不要弄混了。

[ʃ] vs. [s]　she vs. sea / sheet vs. seat / shell vs. sell / shave vs. save

練習 2

◎請聽《Track 45》並在括弧內填入正確答案。

1. Please take your (　　　). / Please take your (　　　).

2. I think (　　　) is very nice. / I think the (　　　) is very nice.

3. I (　　　) my face. / I (　　　) my face.

1. Please take your (seats). / Please take your (sheets).

2. I think (she) is very nice. / I think the (sea) is very nice.

3. I (shaved) my face. / I (saved) my face. （保住面子）

Listening Quiz

◎請聽《Track 43》的會話後回答下面問題。

Nelson 打算之後怎麼辦？

(A) 繼續等待與 Johnson 博士的會面

(B) 參加會議

(C) 回研究室等 Johnson 博士的電話

(D) 4 點以後再打電話給 Johnson 博士

　(C)

會話

 請再聽一次《Track 43》。

A: Hi. Is Dr. Johnson in today?

B: Yes, she is, but she is in a meeting now.

A: When will the meeting be over?

B: I'm not sure, but it won't be over until at least four. What is your name? I'll tell her that you came to see her.

A: My name is Anthony Nelson. I'm from the chemistry lab in the annex.

B: Oh, yes. She mentioned that you were coming in. Give me your phone number and I'll have her call you when she gets out of the meeting.

A: It's extension 7468. Thank you very much.

B: You are welcome.

中譯

A: 你好,請問強森博士在嗎?

B: 她在,不過她現在正在開會。

A: 請問會議什麼時候會結束?

B: 我不太確定,不過至少會開到 4 點左右。請問你貴姓大名?我會將你的到訪轉告給博士知道。

A: 我是附屬大樓化學實驗室的安東尼 · 尼爾森。

B: 喔,對了,博士有說過你今天會來,請留下你的電話號碼,我會請她在會議結束後立刻與你聯絡。

A：我的分機是 7468，謝謝。

B：不客氣。

關鍵字

lab　　研究室，實驗室（laboratory 的縮寫）

annex　　附屬建築物，別館

公事拜訪的說法

請聽《Track 46》。

1. A: Is Dr. Johnson in today?

　 B: Yes, but she is in a meeting now.

2. A: When will the meeting be over?

　 B: I'm not sure, but it won't be over until at least four.

3. A: Give me your phone number and I'll have her call you when she gets out of the meeting.

　 B: It's extension 7468.

解說

● Is Dr. Johnson in today?（請問強森博士在嗎?）這句話裡的 in 有「出勤，上班」的意思。

● over 是「結束」的意思，是表事物結束的英語說法，例如：School will be over at 3:10.（學校上課到 3 點 10 分）。上面原句也可以改說成 When will the meeting finish?

● 「祈使句 + and」是表「請做～，之後…」之意。have her call 的 have 是使役動詞，意思是「使（某人）做～」。使役動詞除 have（命令語意較弱）外，還包括 make（強制命令）、let

（許可）及 get（命令語意較弱）等，其中只有 get 可用「get + 人 + to do」的句型。

練習 1【代換】

請隨《Track 47》做代換練習。

1. Hello. Is Jack   in today?

> Mr. Benson
> Miss Lee
> Professor Watson
> Dr. Fisher

2. When will the meeting   be over?

> the conference
> the lecture
> the demonstration
> the show

練習 2【角色扮演】

請隨《Track 48》在嗶一聲後唸出灰色部分的句子。

1. A: Is Mr. Anderson in today?

   B: Yes, but he is in a meeting now.

2. A: When will the conference be over?

   B: I'm not sure, but it won't be over until at least five.

3. A: Give me your phone number and I'll have him call you when he comes back.

   B: It's extension 3325.

實力測驗

有一天，你碰巧經過友人 Bill 工作的地方，於是心血來潮想去拜訪他，不巧辦公室裡只有他的秘書在，你要怎麼用英語詢問 Bill 在不在呢？

參考解答   Hi. Is Bill in today?

Chapter 9

Future Plans 未來計劃

Listening

Warm-up / Pre-questions

請聽《Track 49》的會話後回答下面問題。

這兩個人正在討論什麼話題?

(A) 新開張的披薩店

(B) 星期五的說明會

(C) 一起外出用餐

解答   (C)

提升聽力的發音技巧

1. 不易區別的音 (3)⋯⋯ [r] 和 [l] ― right vs. light ―

英語的 [r] 和 [l] 的發音極為類似,對東方人來說不易分辨。其實一般說來,[l] 的音聽起來會比 [r] 的音更為響亮。

[r] vs. [l]   right vs. light / read vs. lead / wrong vs. long / pray vs. play

練習 1

請聽《Track 50》並在括弧內填入正確答案。

1. You came at the (   ) time. / I waited for a (   ) time.
2. Please turn on the (   ). / Please turn (   ) at the corner.
3. Let's (   ) now. / Let's (   ) now.

解答 1. You came at the (wrong) time. / I waited for a (long) time.
     2. Please turn on the (light)./Please turn (right) at the corner.
     3. Let's (pray) now. / Let's (play) now.

2. 不易區別的音 (4)⋯⋯母音 [i] 和 [ɪ]　－ leave vs. live －
英語的母音有 20 幾個，數量頗多且有些音很類似，不過若仔細
聽，仍可聽出類似的母音彼此之間的微妙差異，抓住各個母音
的特色。如 [i] 的音不只發得比 [ɪ] 略長，兩者的發音特徵也不同：
[ɪ] 的音其實是比國語注音的「ㄧ」更接近「ㄟ」的音，並且也和
[ɛ] 的音不同。

[i] vs. [ɪ]　leave vs. live / seat vs. sit / meat vs. mitt / heat vs. hit

[ɪ] vs. [ɛ]　pin vs. pen / sit vs. set / did vs. dead / pit vs. pet / wit vs. wet

練習 2

請聽《Track 51》並在括弧內填入正確答案。

1. Please take a (　　). / Please (　　) down.
2. This is a very good (　　). / This is very good (　　).
3. Will you pass me the (　　)? / Will you pass me the (　　)?

解答 1. Please take a (seat). / Please (sit) down.
　　　2. This is a very good (mitt). / This is very good (meat).
　　　3. Will you pass me the (pin)? / WIll you pass me the (pen)?

Listening Quiz

請聽《Track 49》的會話後回答下面問題。

這兩個人明天有甚麼計劃?
　(A) 到新開的餐廳用餐
　(B) 到 Sammy's Wood Fried 披薩店吃晚餐
　(C) 上台報告
　(D) 到以前常玩的地方碰頭

解答　　　　　　　　　　　　　　　　　　　　　　　　　(A)

Speaking

會話

 請再聽一次《Track 49》。

A: Let's go try that new restaurant in Westwood for dinner tonight.

B: Sorry, I can't go. I already have dinner plans.

A: Really? What are you going to do?

B: Some old friends from high school are in town and we are going to our old hangout.

A: Where is that?

B: Sammy's Wood Fried Pizza.

A: Okay. Then can we go tomorrow?

B: Sure, I can go tomorrow, but I need to finish preparing my presentation for Friday and won't be able to leave until it's done.

A: All right. When will you be finished?

B: Probably at seven o'clock.

A: Shall we meet at the restaurant at 7:30, then?

B: 7:30 sounds good. See you then.

中譯

A: 今晚要不要一起去西木新開幕的那家餐廳試試口味？

B: 抱歉，我不能去。今天晚餐我另外有約了。

A: 是嗎？你有什麼計劃？

B: 我有一些高中死黨到城裡來了,所以我們要去我們的老地方吃飯。

A: 喔,你們的「老地方」是哪兒?

B: Sammy's Wood 披薩店。

A: OK,那麼明天去可以嗎?

B: 沒問題,明天我有空,不過我必須先準備好禮拜五的上台報告才能離開公司。

A: 好,你大約什麼時候能做完?

B: 差不多 7 點左右。

A: 那麼我們約 7 點半在餐廳見面,好嗎?

B: 7 點半沒問題,到時候見!

關鍵字

hangout　聚集處,老地方

邀請的說法

 請聽《Track 52》。

1. A: Let's go try that new restaurant in Westwood for dinner tonight.

   B: Yes, let's. They say it's a very good restaurant.

2. A: Shall we meet at the restaurant at 7:30, then?

   B: 7:30 sounds good. See you then.

3. A: How about having lunch at the Plaza?

   B: That's a good idea. Let's do it.

● Let's～是「一起做～吧」的意思，是邀請、提議的句型。同意對方的邀約時用 Yes, let's. 回答；要回拒則回答 No, let's not.。而「去做～」的 go and do 在美式講法中，通常會省略 and，簡單用 go do 表達，如原句的 go try 即是 go and try 的省略。

● Shall we～? 也是邀請、提議的句型，是「～好嗎」之意。回答時和回應 Let's～引導的邀請句相同，可以回答 Yes, let's. 或 No, let's not.。

● 邀請的說法除了 Let's～和 Shall we～? 之外，也可以用 How about + V.ing?（做～好嗎）表達。另外，「How about + 名詞」是「～怎麼樣」之意，如 How about a snack?（要不要來份零嘴?）。

練習 1 【代換】

 請隨《Track 53》做代換練習。

1. Let's play tennis this afternoon.

> go to the movies tonight.
> eat out tonight.
> go see what they are doing.
> go try that new restaurant for dinner tonight.

2. Shall we go now?

> go in this restaurant?
> stop at McDonald's for lunch?
> go see the house?
> go get the book?

練習 2【角色扮演】

請隨《Track 54》在嗶一聲後唸出灰色部分的句子。

1. A: Let's go try the new Italian restaurant for dinner tonight.

   B: Yes, let's. They say it's a very good restaurant.

2. A: Shall we meet in the lobby at six o'clock, then?

   B: Six o'clock sounds good. See you then.

3. A: How about having dinner at the Olympia Plaza?

   B: That's a good idea. Let's do it.

實力測驗

今天是發薪水的日子，荷包滿滿的你想邀同事 Tom 下班後一起小酌一番，你要如何開口邀請他呢？

參考解答　　　　　　　Tom, let's go for a drink after work.

Chapter 10	Telephone Calls	打電話

Listening

Warm-up / Pre-questions

請聽《Track 55》的會話後回答下面問題。

這個男人打電話到哪裡?

  (A) Kurt 公司

  (B) Higgins 先生的公司

  (C) Higgins 先生的家

解答   (B)

提升聽力的發音技巧

1. 不易區別的音 (5)⋯⋯母音 [æ] 和 [ʌ] —back vs. buck—

英語的母音如 [æ] [ʌ] [ɑ] [ə] 聽起來都很像國語注音的「ㄚ」,其實這些音彼此之間仍有微妙的差異,我們可以依嘴巴開合度的大小抓住它們的發音特徵。

[æ] vs. [ʌ]　back vs. buck / hat vs. hut / cap vs. cup / cat vs. cut

[ɑ] vs. [ʌ]　hot vs. hut / pot vs. putt / cot vs. cut / got vs. gut

[ɑr] vs. [ɝ]　hard vs. heard / heart vs. hurt / star vs. stir

練習 1

請聽《Track 56》並在括弧內填入正確答案。

  1. Pass me the (　　　), please. / Pass me the (　　　), please.

  2. That was a very nice (　　　). / That was a very nice (　　　).

  3. She has a kind (　　　). / She was badly (　　　).

解答　1. Pass me the (cup), please. / Pass me the (cap), please.

2. That was a very nice (pot). / That was a very nice (putt).

3. She has a kind (heart). / She was badly (hurt).

2. 不易區別的音 (6)……母音 [ɔ] 和 [o]　— call vs. coal —

英語的 [ɔ] 和 [o] 聽起來很像國語注音的「ㄡ」，要分清楚似乎有些困難。其實 [ɔ] 是略同國語「ㄚ」與「ㄛ」之間的音；[o] 則是發接近「ㄡ」的音之後，再漸漸轉為「ㄨ」的音。

[ɔ] vs. [o]　call vs. coal / bought vs. boat / hall vs. hole / called vs. cold / law vs. low / raw vs. row / saw vs. sew

練習 2

請聽《Track 57》並在括弧內填入正確答案。

1. I gave him a toy (　　). / I (　　) him a toy.

2. It's a big (　　). / It's a big (　　).

3. She's studying (　　). / She's feeling (　　).

解答　　　　1. I gave him a toy (boat). / I (bought) him a toy.

2. It's a big (hole). / It's a big (hall).

3. She's studying (law). / She's feeling (low).

Listening Quiz

請聽《Track 55》的會話後回答下面問題。

Spencer 先生打算一個小時後做什麼？

(A) 拜訪 Higgins 先生　　　(B) 再打一次電話給 Higgins 先生

(C) 等 Higgins 先生回電　　(D) 等 Higgins 先生的留言

解答　　　　　　　　　　　　　　　　　　　　　(B)

Speaking

會話

請再聽一次《Track 55》。

A: Emerson Technology. May I help you?

B: Hello. This is Mr. Robert Spencer of Kurt Company. May I speak to Mr. Higgins, please?

A: I'm sorry, Mr. Higgins isn't in just now. Can I take a message?

B: Well, ah, will he be back in the office soon?

A: Yes, I suppose so.

B: Well, then, will you tell him that I'll call again in an hour, around 11 o'clock?

A: Sure, Mr. Spencer.

B: Thank you.

A: You're welcome.

中譯

A: 艾默森科技公司。您好，我能為您服務嗎？

B: 你好，我是克特公司的羅伯特‧史賓賽，請幫我接希金氏先生。

A: 抱歉，希金氏先生現在不在，我可以幫您留言嗎？

B: 喔，請問希金氏先生會很快回到辦公室嗎？

A: 應該會。

B: 那麼能否請你轉告他，我會在一個小時後，大約 11 點鐘再打來。

A: 沒問題，史賓賽先生。

B: 謝謝你。

A: 不客氣。

打電話的說法

請聽《Track 58》。

1. A: Hello. May I speak to Mr. Higgins, please?
   B: Speaking.
2. A: Who's calling, please?
   B: This is Mr. Spencer of Kurt Company calling.
3. A: Mr. Higgins is on the other line right now. Would you like
      him to call you back?
   B: Yes, please. My phone number is 323-465-7698.

解說

● 打電話時，通常會先開口說 May I speak to～?（麻煩你，我要
  找～）；接電話者若剛好是對方要找的人，可以回答 Speaking.
  或 This is he/she.。

● 接電話者若要問明「你是哪一位?」時，可用 Who's calling? 或
  Who's speaking? 詢問；打電話的人可以回答如 This is Clark
  speaking. 的句子。

● be on the other line 的意思是「正在講其他電話」。

練習 1【代換】

請隨《Track 59》做代換練習。

1. Hello. May I speak to Jim?

> Grace?
> Mr. Robinson?
> Miss Miller?
> Mr. Williams of the sales department?

2. This is Tom   speaking.

> Kate
> Jim Brown
> Nancy Peterson
> Kent Adams of the sales department

練習 2【角色扮演】

 請隨《Track 60》在嗶一聲後唸出灰色部分的句子。

1. A: Hello. May I speak to Ms. Walker, please?

   B: Speaking.

2. A: Who's calling, please?

   B: This is Mr. Kim of MAX Communications calling.

3. A: Ms. Powell is on the other line right now. Would you like her to call you back?

   B: Yes, please. My phone number is 854-765-4680.

實力測驗

> 你的名字是 Richard Lee，是 Nelcom Company 的職員，正打電話到 Marshall, Inc. 找 Laura Scott 小姐。現在電話的另一頭傳來 Marshall, Inc. May I help you? 的聲音，你要如何用英語回應呢？

> 參考解答　Hello. This is Richard Lee of Nelcom Campany. May I speak to Miss Laura Scott, please?

自然學習英語動詞——基礎篇

大西泰斗、Paul C. McVay 著 ／ 何月華 譯

英語一個動詞動輒八、九個語義,若是硬生生地背誦每一個語義實在不是個好方法。本書以圖畫式的「意象學習法」,幫助你不需過度依賴文字解釋,就能清楚區分每個字彙特有的語感,切實掌握各個字彙不同的涵義,使你脫離機械式死背中文翻譯的夢魘,輕鬆暢遊英語動詞的世界。

自然學習英語動詞——進階篇

大西泰斗、Paul C. McVay 著 ／ 林韓菁 譯

本書延續《自然學習英語動詞——基礎篇》的精神,從各個進階動詞的語感出發,藉由親身體會各個動詞所具有的原型意象,幫助你靈活運用英語動詞的各種用法,掌握以英語為母語者的語感。當你把英語語感調整成和外國人士一樣時,脫口說英語將是再自然也不過的事了。

英語喜怒哀樂開口說

大內 博
大內ジャネット 著／何信彰 譯

附CD

你是不是「高興的時候」只會用happy、「悲傷的時候」只會用sad，再加上一緊張就什麼話都說不出來呢？我們要如何用英語確切地表達出自己的情感呢？本書依各種不同的場合並搭配如臨實境的對話範例，教你記住適當的英語說法及其之間微妙的差異，讓你能確實感受對方心境，也能豐富自我情感表現的色彩！

黛安的日記1

Ronald Brown 著／呂亨英 譯

大家都知道，學好英文並不是一件容易輕鬆的事，對年僅九歲、從未接觸過英文的黛安更是如此。本書以流暢道地的英文創作，輔以中肯自然的中譯，記錄一位台灣小女孩的英語學習探險。想不想知道一位完全不懂英文的小女孩如何在美國生存？請來看看這本書吧！

國家圖書館出版品預行編目資料

英語聽&說:入門篇 / 白野伊津夫, Lisa A. Stefani著;
　沈薇譯. －－初版二刷. －－臺北市: 三民, 2004
　　面;　　公分

　ISBN 957-14-3746-8 (精裝)

　1.英國語言－讀本

805.18　　　　　　　　　　　　　　　92003147

網路書店位址　http://www.sanmin.com.tw

© 英語聽&說
—— 入門篇

著作人　白野伊津夫　Lisa A. Stefani
譯　者　沈　薇
發行人　劉振強
著作財
產權人　三民書局股份有限公司
　　　　臺北市復興北路386號
發行所　三民書局股份有限公司
　　　　地址 / 臺北市復興北路386號
　　　　電話 / (02)25006600
　　　　郵撥 / 0009998-5
印刷所　三民書局股份有限公司
門市部　復北店 / 臺北市復興北路386號
　　　　重南店 / 臺北市重慶南路一段61號
初版一刷　2003年4月
初版二刷　2004年7月
編　號　S 804341
基本定價　肆元貳角
行政院新聞局登記證局版臺業字第○二○○號

有著作權‧不准侵害

ISBN　957-14-3746-8　(精裝)

白野伊津夫

日本明海大學副教授、明治大學講師。美國維吉尼亞大學口語傳播（Speech Communication）研究所碩士。著有多本與英語學習相關的書籍。

Lisa A. Stefani

美國加州 Grossmont College 講師。聖地牙哥州立大學碩士。亦有多本英語學習的相關著作問世。

《入門篇》CD Track 【全片英語錄製／長約 56 分鐘／共 60 個 Track】

Track 1 ～ 6　　　Chapter 1: Greeting
　　　　　　　　（第 1 章：問候）

Track 7 ～ 12　　Chapter 2: Introduction
　　　　　　　　（第 2 章：介紹）

Track 13 ～ 18　Chapter 3: Asking For Permission
　　　　　　　　（第 3 章：請求許可）

Track 19 ～ 24　Chapter 4: Requests
　　　　　　　　（第 4 章：提出要求）

Track 25 ～ 30　Chapter 5: Asking Questions
　　　　　　　　（第 5 章：詢問）

Track 31 ～ 36　Chapter 6: Enjoying Food
　　　　　　　　（第 6 章：享受美食）

Track 37 ～ 42　Chapter 7: What Did You Do Today?
　　　　　　　　（第 7 章：你今天做了什麼？）

Track 43 ～ 48　Chapter 8: Is Dr. Johnson In Today?
　　　　　　　　（第 8 章：請問強森博士在嗎？）

Track 49 ～ 54　Chapter 9: Future Plans
　　　　　　　　（第 9 章：未來計劃）

Track 55 ～ 60　Chapter 10: Telephone Calls
　　　　　　　　（第 10 章：打電話）